Grandmother Winter

Phyllis Root   *Pictures by Beth Krommes*

Houghton Mifflin Company
Boston

The text of this book is set in Horley Oldstyle.
The illustrations are scratchboard, hand tinted with watercolors.

Library of Congress Cataloging-in-Publication Data
Root, Phyllis.
Grandmother Winter / Phyllis Root ; illustrated by Beth Krommes.
p. cm.
Summary: When Grandmother Winter shakes out her feather quilt
birds, bats, bears, and other creatures prepare themselves for the cold.
RNF ISBN 0-395-88399-7 PAP ISBN 0-618-49485-5
[1. Winter — Fiction. 2. Snow — Fiction. 3. Animals — Fiction.]
I. Krommes, Beth, ill. II. Title.
PZ7.R6784Gp   1999
[E] — dc21   98-50515 CIP AC

Manufactured in the United States of America
WOZ 10 9 8 7 6 5

For my friend Barbara
—P.R.

For my mother, in her memory
—B.K.

Grandmother Winter lives all alone
with her snow-white flock of geese.

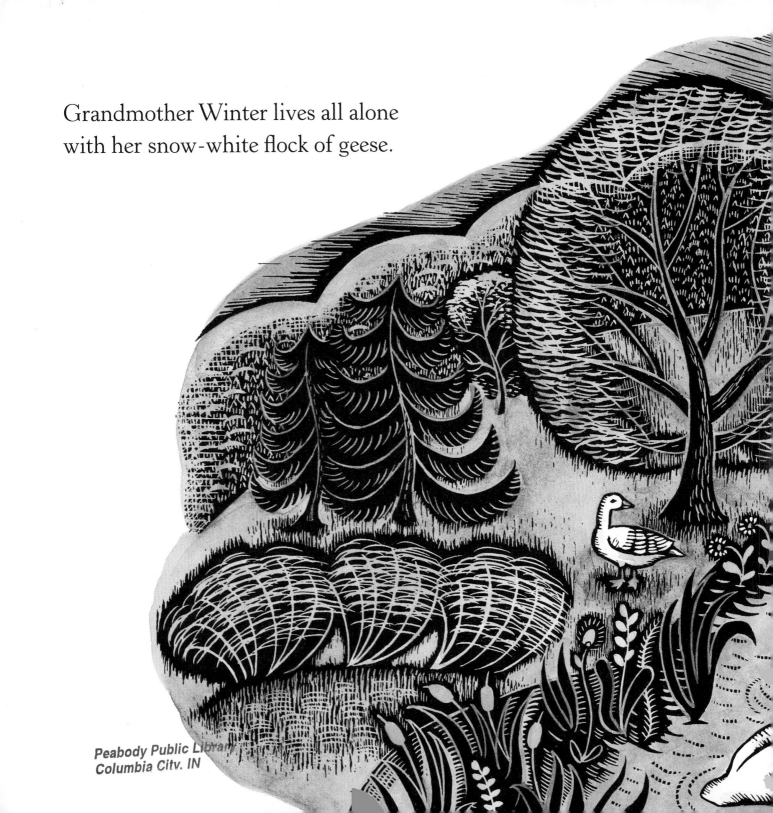

All spring
Grandmother herds her geese
as they gabble and squawk,
honk and hiss,
flapping a storm of feathers.

All through the summer
Grandmother gathers the feathers,
soft as snowflakes,
bright as a winter moon.

Come autumn,
Grandmother sews on her quilt
stitch by stitch,
stuffing it full of feathers.

When the days burn down
toward the longest night
Grandmother shakes her feather quilt.

Flake by flake
the snow begins to fall.

When Grandmother shakes her quilt
children come running from their homes,
catching snowflakes cold on their tongues.

Grown-ups build their wood piles high
and scurry for sweaters and mittens and skis.

When Grandmother shakes her feather quilt
cardinals and chickadees
fluff themselves up
against the cold.

Snowshoe hares and weasels
put on their coats of white.

When Grandmother shakes her feather quilt
earthworms tunnel deep in the dirt.
Brown bats hang head-down,
bundled in blankets of wings.

Under leaves and in hollow logs
mourning cloak butterflies sleep.

Below the milky ice of the pond pickerel frogs and painted turtles bury themselves in mud.

Minnows and sunfish slowly swim.

When Grandmother shakes her feather quilt
bull snakes coil in old woodchuck dens.
In prairie mounds and clumps of weeds
jumping mice wrap their tails round
and close their eyes.

When Grandmother shakes her quilt
black bears yawn,
and burrow into hillside dens.

Children pull off boots and coats,
tumble into bed to be tucked in.
All night they will dream
of flying over hills
and making angel wings
in the snow.

Grandmother gives her feather quilt
one last shake,
blows out the candle,
and climbs into bed.

The wind in the pine
sings *shush, shush.*

What does Grandmother Winter do then?
Under her quilt,
thick as a snowfall,
warm as a flock of geese,
Grandmother Winter sleeps
while the days drift down like feathers.

And Grandmother's geese,
what will they do?

Heads tucked under wings,
they will wait until spring

to gabble and squawk,
honk and hiss,
flapping a new storm of feathers.